With special thanks to Natalie Doherty

For Nic, Steph, Joe, Iain, and Frankie x

Text Copyright © 2013 by Hothouse Fiction
Illustrations Copyright © 2013 by Sophy Williams

ISBN 978-1-338-08245-6

10 9 8 7 6 5 4 3 2 1   17 18 19 20 21

Printed in the U.S.A.   40
First printing 2017

Book design by Mary Claire Cruz

The
Playful
Panda

Amelia Cobb

Illustrated by Sophy Williams

Scholastic Inc.

Chapter One

A Treat for Daisy

Zoe Parker grinned as she raced down
the path. It was Saturday morning at
the Rescue Zoo, and Zoe was on her
way to visit some of her favorite animals.
Halfway down the path she stopped at
a wooden gate and reached for the pretty
silver paw-print charm on her necklace.

This was no ordinary necklace—it

opened the door to every single enclosure in the Rescue Zoo! It had been a present from her great-uncle Horace, who had built the zoo, and Zoe never took it off. She held the charm against a small panel on the gate and, with a quiet click, it swung open.

Zoe walked into a warm, wide plain, covered in tall grass and lush trees. Just beyond the gate was the house where the giraffes slept, a tall redbrick building with a high arched doorway. Zoe shaded her eyes from the sunshine and saw the herd gathered at the other end of the enclosure, drinking from a sparkling stream. By the gate stood a wheelbarrow full of fresh straw, and a large garden rake. The giraffe-keeper, Frankie, had promised Zoe she could help out this morning, and everything she needed was ready for her!

Zoe grabbed the wheelbarrow and
pushed it into the giraffe house. She
picked up the rake and began lifting the
straw out, spreading it carefully on the
ground so that the giraffes would have
clean, comfortable bedding that night.

She hummed happily as she worked, enjoying the warm breeze and wondering where her best friend had gone. He had dashed off along the path in front of her that morning, too excited to slow down!

Suddenly the straw in the wheelbarrow started to wriggle. Zoe watched curiously as it shook from side to side. Then a furry little head popped out and a pair of huge golden eyes blinked playfully at her.

"Meep!" Zoe laughed. "There you are, you naughty thing!"

With a cheerful chirp, the tiny creature

sprang out of the wheelbarrow and climbed up onto Zoe's shoulder, sending bits of straw everywhere. Meep was a gray mouse lemur. He was very small with a long curling tail and soft, delicate ears that stuck up in the air. He'd come to the zoo when he was just a baby, and lived with Zoe and her mom in their cottage.

"I wondered where you'd disappeared to, Meep. You're supposed to be helping me clean the giraffe enclosure, not making a mess!" Zoe shook her head but couldn't help smiling. The little lemur was so cute that she could never *really* be mad at him.

As she finished spreading out the straw, Zoe heard a gentle bray behind her and turned around. The youngest member of the giraffe herd, Daisy, had come over to

greet them. She was just a few months old
but she was still more than twice as tall
as Zoe!

"Morning, Daisy!" called Zoe. The
graceful giraffe trotted over, and Zoe put
down her rake and reached up to stroke
Daisy's long, slender neck. Every giraffe
had a different pattern of special
markings that helped Zoe tell them apart.
She knew this was Daisy from the pretty
star shape on her forehead.

"Wow, Mom! Look!" cried an excited
voice from the path. "A baby giraffe—
and there's a girl petting her!"

The zoo gates must have opened to the
public while Zoe was working, because
a family of visitors had walked up to
the fence. A lady was pushing a bright-
blue stroller with a toddler sitting inside,

clapping his little hands happily. Next to them was a red-haired girl a little younger than Zoe, wearing a giraffe T-shirt. She was gazing in amazement at Zoe and Daisy. Zoe smiled at her, and Meep chattered a friendly greeting.

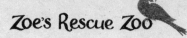

The girl smiled back shyly, her eyes wide. "Are you a zookeeper?" she asked Zoe.

Zoe giggled. "Maybe one day!" she said. "I'm Zoe, and this is Daisy. My great-uncle Horace is the owner of the Rescue Zoo."

"Oh, you mean Horace Higgins! I've heard of him," said the girl's mom.

"He's a famous explorer, isn't he?" her dad added.

Zoe nodded. "He met so many hurt, lost, or frightened animals on his adventures that he decided to build the Rescue Zoo. Now it's a safe place for any creature that needs a home," she explained. "Great-Uncle Horace still travels around the world looking for animals to help. Sometimes he's away for months, and we never know when he's going to come back.

"My mom's the Rescue Zoo vet. We live in a little cottage here in the zoo, so she can treat any animal whenever they need her. And I spend as much time with the animals as I can, especially on the weekends!"

"I can't believe you *live* here," the girl said wistfully. "You're so lucky."

"I know," said Zoe, beaming. She was very proud of her special home!

"And are the giraffes your favorites?" the girl's mom asked. "Amy here *loves* giraffes. She was so excited about seeing them, so this is the first enclosure we came to."

Zoe smiled. "Would you like to feed Daisy?" she asked. "She's already had a lot of acacia leaves for breakfast, but I have an apple here that you can give her as a treat."

Amy's mouth dropped open. "Really?" she breathed. "I would *love* to!"

Zoe reached into her pocket and passed a shiny green apple over the fence. Amy clutched it, looking nervous. "Just hold your arm out straight and keep your hand flat. She won't bite. She's really gentle," Zoe promised, smiling at Daisy.

Amy's dad pulled out his camera and started taking pictures as Amy held the apple out. Very carefully, Daisy bent her long neck and sniffed the little girl's hand. Then she picked up the apple in one bite and started crunching it happily. Amy gasped. "Her nose is so soft!" she whispered.

"Did she come from somewhere in Africa?" Amy's dad asked.

Zoe shook her head. "Daisy's mom, Dolly, was rescued from Kenya. But Daisy was born here in the zoo, in the middle of the night. I was the first person to see her! Meep and I came to give Dolly her breakfast in the morning, and there was Daisy—already walking around!"

When Amy had finished giving Daisy her treat, her dad ruffled her hair. "We'd better go and visit some of the other animals now, Amy. We've still got a lot to see," he told her. "How about the hippos next?"

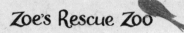

"We'll come back to see Daisy before we leave," her mom added.

Amy grinned at Zoe. "Thank you *so* much for letting me feed her. I loved it," she said, her cheeks pink with happiness.

The family walked off down the path, chatting excitedly. Zoe waited until they were out of sight, then sighed. "That was close!" she said to Daisy. "I didn't hear them walking up to the fence. It's lucky we weren't talking!"

Daisy nodded, and Meep squeaked in agreement. "They might have guessed our secret, Zoe!" the little lemur chirped.

Zoe grinned. Most people thought her life was amazing because she lived at the Rescue Zoo. But there was something else unusual about her—only this was a secret. On her sixth birthday Zoe had found out

that animals talk to people all the time!
Most people just hear squeaks, grunts,
roars, and other animal noises. But some
people can understand everything they
say. Lucky, special people—like Zoe!

Chapter Two
A Double Delivery

"Come on, Meep!" said Zoe. "Let's head to the otter enclosure. Mom said the babies are getting a new toy this morning!"

Daisy bleated gently at Zoe, who smiled. "Of course we'll see you later," she promised, reaching out to stroke Daisy's soft muzzle. "Frankie told me you've been playing chase with the rest of the herd, and I want to come and watch."

Daisy bleated again and fluttered her long, dark eyelashes. Zoe giggled and nodded. "OK," she said. "If you're *very* good, I might bring another apple with me." The young giraffe grunted happily and trotted back to the rest of the herd.

Zoe made sure the gate was safely locked before heading down the path. It was a warm fall day and the zoo was busy with visitors. Meep scampered along in front of her, darting nimbly through the crowds and along the top of the fences. Some people pointed, and one lady gasped, "Look! That monkey has escaped from its enclosure!"

Zoe giggled. "Don't worry," she called. "Meep's not a monkey, he's a lemur, and he hasn't escaped. He's one of the most special animals at the Rescue Zoo and he's allowed to run free."

They passed the colorful kingfishers perched around their leafy lake home and the capuchin monkeys in their lush jungle. There was an especially big crowd gathered in front of the next enclosure. Luna was a beautiful arctic wolf with a soft, shaggy white coat, a jet-black nose, and pale-blue eyes. Last month her gorgeous cubs had been born: a girl named Stella and a boy named Sam. Their home was a snowy clearing, surrounded by a circle of pine trees glittering with ice, with a gap at the front for visitors to look through. Luna and Sam were curled up asleep together, but little Stella was wide awake and playing happily with her mom's fluffy tail. When she saw Zoe, she barked and rushed up to the fence. Zoe waved at her. If the paths had been quieter, she would have stopped to speak to the cub, but with so many visitors around it was too risky.

A little farther along was another
beautiful enclosure—but this one was
empty. It was full of bamboo plants with
a waterfall trickling down a rocky cliff.
Three low wooden platforms were built
in the middle, connected by ladders and
ramps. This used to be the home of Su
Lin, the giant panda.

Zoe couldn't help feeling sad as she
walked past the empty enclosure. Su Lin
had died a few months ago. Zoe's mom
had explained that Su Lin wasn't hurt
or sick—she was just very old. Zoe had
cried for ages but tried to remember that
Su Lin had loved her life at the Rescue
Zoo. She had been a gentle, cuddly
creature, full of funny stories about
growing up in China with her little sister,
Bai Yun. Zoe bit her lip and glanced at

 18

Meep, who jumped into her arms for a hug. They both missed the giant panda very much.

Once they turned the corner and saw
the otter enclosure ahead, Zoe felt more
cheerful. Noisy squeaks of excitement
were coming from their riverside home.

Zoe ran up to the fence, and Meep
scampered onto Zoe's head for a better
view. Jess, the otter-keeper, was holding
a yellow bouncy ball above her head.
The baby otters, Otto and Benedict, were
waiting on the riverbank, eagerly bobbing
their sleek little heads up and down.
Then Jess threw the ball into the water,
and with a splash Otto and Benedict

jumped right after it! Otto reached the ball first and sent it high up into the air with a clever flick of his snout. His brother squeaked happily and turned a somersault under the water. "That looks like fun!" Zoe called, laughing.

Suddenly Meep's ears pricked up. "What's that noise, Zoe?" the little lemur asked.

Zoe listened. Over the squeaks and splashes of the otters she could hear a strange honking sound. "I don't know, Meep," she said, puzzled. "It's a little like when some of the geese caught a cold last year."

"Or when Oscar tied his trunk into a knot by accident," Meep suggested, giggling.

"I don't think it's an animal sound at all," Zoe said thoughtfully. "It sounds more like . . . a car horn playing a funny tune. But how would anyone drive a car into the Rescue Zoo? The paths aren't wide enough!"

The noise was growing louder now, and Zoe could hear the low grumble of an engine. Otto and Benedict were peering curiously over the fence. In the trees above them, a flock of wild green parakeets started squawking excitedly.

Suddenly a huge gleaming motorcycle appeared from around the corner. With another honk of its horn, it sped down the path toward them. The driver was

wearing a big shiny helmet, a safari
jacket, and a pair of old-fashioned
goggles. A white scarf was wrapped
around his neck. Meep squeaked with joy
and Zoe gasped. "Great-Uncle Horace!"

With a screech of brakes, the motorcycle
pulled up next to them. Its license plate
said RESCUE 1 and it was covered with
colorful stickers, showing all the places
in the world that Great-Uncle Horace
had visited. Attached to it was a bright-
red sidecar with the hot air balloon
symbol of the Rescue Zoo painted on the
side. A large and very grumpy-looking
bird was perched inside it, her blue
feathers fluffed up. Kiki was Great-Uncle
Horace's hyacinth macaw, and they
went everywhere together, just like Zoe
and Meep!

Great-Uncle Horace lifted off his goggles and beamed at them, his untidy white hair sticking out from underneath his helmet. "Zoe, my dear. And Meep, you little rascal! It's wonderful to see you both. I've missed you very much."

"Hooray! Hooray! Goo's back!" chattered Meep. The funny little lemur found it hard to say Great-Uncle

Horace's name so had made up his own version instead.

"We've missed you too," said Zoe, grinning. "I can't believe you're home, Great-Uncle Horace. We thought you were somewhere in Asia!"

"I *was* in Asia, my dear. Northern China, to be precise. And I've brought a very important delivery back to the zoo!" Great-Uncle Horace's eyes twinkled. "I came as fast as I could, by boat and then by bike. That's why Kiki here is rather cranky. We drove along some very bumpy roads, you see. Motorcycle is *not* her favorite way to travel."

Meep snickered and Kiki gave a haughty squawk. The silly lemur and the proud old bird loved each other's owners, but they didn't like each other very much!

"Naughty Meep," whispered Zoe.

"Anyway, my dear, hop on!" said Great-Uncle Horace.

"Where are we going?" Zoe asked. As she climbed onto the motorcycle behind Great-Uncle Horace, with Meep on her shoulder, she spotted a large wooden crate tucked into the sidecar next to Kiki. What could it be? Great-Uncle Horace had mentioned *a very important delivery*. Zoe's heart leaped. *Please let it be a new animal for the Rescue Zoo!* she thought hopefully.

"Oh, not far," said Great-Uncle Horace, smiling mysteriously. "Hold tight!"

The engine roared and they raced back along the path. All around them the air was filled with happy squawks, whinnies, and hoots as the news that Great-Uncle Horace was back spread through the zoo.

They turned the corner and parked at the side of the path, underneath a sprawling plum tree. "Zoe, look where Goo has brought us," Meep whispered in Zoe's ear.

"Su Lin's empty enclosure!" Zoe gasped. She glanced at the wooden crate. Suddenly her heart was racing with excitement.

Great-Uncle Horace took off his helmet and turned to Zoe. "I know you must be wondering what I've brought home with me, my dear," he said, smiling. "Well, it *is* a new animal for the zoo—and we already have the perfect home for it. Can you guess what it is?"

Meep bounced up and down on Zoe's shoulder. "I know! I know!" the little lemur chirped.

27

Zoe took a deep, nervous breath. She thought she knew too—and she desperately hoped she was right. "Is it . . . is it a panda?" she asked, crossing her fingers tightly.

Great-Uncle Horace shook his head. Meep squeaked in surprise, and Zoe's heart sank in disappointment. As soon as they had arrived at Su Lin's enclosure, she'd been *sure* it was a panda.

Then Zoe realized Great-Uncle Horace was chuckling softly. He climbed off the motorcycle and helped Zoe and Meep down too. Kiki flew out of the sidecar and landed in the plum tree overhead, making a few golden leaves drift gently to the ground. Then Great-Uncle Horace reached over and opened the door of the wooden crate slightly. "Have a look," he told her.

Zoe peeked inside. It was warm and snug in the crate, and she could make out a fluffy black-and-white bundle. The bundle wriggled—and Zoe grinned in delight. There were *two* adorable creatures, cuddled up asleep together. "I can't believe it!" she cried. "It's not a panda. It's *two* pandas!"

"That's right!" said Great-Uncle Horace, beaming happily. "Two baby panda cubs. They're just three months old—and they're sisters. Zoe, meet the Rescue Zoo's first ever panda twins!"

Chapter Three
Zoe's Mistake

Zoe stared in delight at the fluffy bundles. One of the sleeping cubs rolled over and yawned, showing her tiny pink tongue, before snuggling back up against her sister.

"They're beautiful," Zoe said softly. "Where did they come from?"

"From another zoo," Great-Uncle

Horace explained. "Twin pandas are very rare indeed, Zoe. But it costs a lot of money to look after just one panda, because they need so much special care. The zoo could only afford to keep one cub and was going to send her sister to a panda orphanage."

Zoe frowned. "But that's horrible! They're twins; they belong together."

"Exactly, my dear!" cried Great-Uncle Horace, nodding. "That's why I decided to bring them both to the Rescue Zoo. It was the only way to make sure they weren't split up." He glanced at the enclosure, then smiled at Zoe gently. "Besides, I knew how much everyone was missing Su Lin. Of course, the twins can never replace her. But when I had the chance to bring pandas back to the zoo, I just had to take it!"

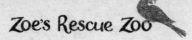

"I'm glad you did," Zoe replied, grinning. Meep chattered in agreement, and Zoe smiled at her little friend.

"Well, I'd better tell everyone else," said Great-Uncle Horace. He rummaged around in the pockets of his safari jacket. Zoe giggled as he pulled out a ball of string, then a compass, and then a pack of his favorite cookies. In the largest pocket he found his battered old safari hat, which he jammed onto his head. Finally he held up what he had been looking for: a walkie-talkie.

"Come in, Rescue Zoo," he announced happily. "Horace speaking! I'm back, and I'm at the panda enclosure with Zoe and Meep. Come quickly, everyone. I've brought two panda cubs with me!"

32

There was a crackle, then the zoo staff all started replying. "Mr. Higgins! That's fantastic news!" Zoe heard Jess say from the otter enclosure.

"I'll be there in a minute!" added the penguin-keeper, Will.

The most excited reply was from Stephanie, the keeper who had looked after Su Lin. "Pandas?" she gasped. "Two of them? I can't believe it! Wait there— I'm coming right over."

There was another crackle, and Zoe heard a familiar, happy voice. "Uncle Horace, I'm so pleased you're home," cried her mom. "I'm on my way now. Don't run off on another adventure before I get there!"

Great-Uncle Horace chuckled. "Ah, there's my favorite niece. Don't worry,

my dear. This time I'll be staying at
the zoo for a few days, to help our new
arrivals settle in."

Great-Uncle Horace turned back to
Zoe. "Let's take the twins into their new
home," he said. "They must be hungry.
Did you know that pandas spend more
than half of every day eating? And do
you know what they love to eat more
than anything else?"

"Bamboo!" Zoe said. Su Lin had
munched through dozens of pieces of
hard green bamboo every day.

"That's right!" said Great-Uncle
Horace. "Bamboo's a fascinating plant,
Zoe. It grows very quickly indeed, and
there are more than three hundred
different types. Here at the Rescue Zoo,
we have just three kinds: umbrella, arrow,

and golden bamboo. Our new arrivals are still a little too young for bamboo though. For now, we'll feed them lots of nice, warm milk."

Carefully, Great-Uncle Horace lifted the crate out of the sidecar and carried it over to the enclosure. Zoe opened the gate with her paw-print charm, and they all went inside. Most of the Rescue Zoo's enclosures were kept neat and tidy, but this one had become very overgrown since Su Lin died. Chinese wildflowers had sprung up among the trees, and with no one there to nibble the bamboo plants they'd grown right up to the top of the fence.

"Goodness!" exclaimed Great-Uncle Horace. "It feels very wild indeed, as if we really are in the Chinese mountains.

How nice! Now, let's see what our new arrivals think."

He put the crate down and opened the door all the way, so it rested on the ground. Then he stepped back and waited. Zoe watched the crate and tried not to fidget. When an animal was seeing its new home for the first time, the Rescue Zoo staff were always as quiet and still as possible. That way, the animal wouldn't be frightened. Zoe didn't move, even though she was so excited. Naughty Meep couldn't be still for a second and hopped up and down, desperate to see what the pandas did.

Everything was quiet. Then there was a curious squeak from inside the crate. The cubs had noticed the open door!

Suddenly a little face appeared in the

doorway. Zoe gasped as she saw the first cub, now wide awake. Her face and body were as white and fluffy as a cloud. Her ears, arms, and legs were black, and there was a ring of black fur around each of her bright, curious eyes. Her black nose twitched, and she scampered out of the crate excitedly.

"I think she likes it, don't you?" whispered Great-Uncle Horace, beaming.

Zoe nodded, unable to tear her eyes away from the beautiful animal.

Then the second cub peeked out shyly. She was a little smaller than her sister, with a black patch on her tummy. She gazed at the lush trees, the glittering waterfall, and the tall bamboo plants. Then she put her little head to one side and curiously squeaked a question.

"Yes, that's right!" Zoe burst out excitedly. "This is your new home— the Rescue Zoo."

Both cubs stared at her in

surprise. By her feet, Meep squealed in horror. "Zoe, shhhh!" the little lemur hissed. "Goo's here!"

Zoe clapped her hand tightly over her mouth, as if she could somehow make the words disappear. Suddenly her heart was racing. She couldn't *believe* she'd made such a silly mistake. *She had talked to the pandas in front of Great-Uncle Horace!*

Chapter Four
A Lucky Escape

Zoe looked quickly at Great-Uncle Horace. She had never spoken to an animal in front of another person before, but she'd been so excited about the pandas, she'd forgotten Great-Uncle Horace was there! She thought desperately, trying not to panic. What could she say to explain? Maybe she could pretend she'd muddled up her words?

But Great-Uncle Horace didn't seem to have heard her. There was a funny smile on his face, but he was still watching the cubs look around their new home. Zoe let out a deep, shaky breath. *That was a lucky escape!* she thought. *I need to be more careful.*

"Gosh, Zoe, you look very serious," cried a voice from behind her. "Cheer up, sweetheart! This is the best day we've had at Rescue Zoo in ages. I can't believe we have panda twins!"

It was Stephanie, Su Lin's old keeper, her freckled face pink from rushing down the path. Her chestnut-brown hair was tied up in a bun, and she was wearing the blue Rescue Zoo uniform with a golden hot air balloon sewn on the pocket. She grinned in delight, crouching down to stroke the smaller cub's soft fur. "Aren't they *beautiful*! I don't think I've ever seen such small pandas before."

Will, Jess, and Frankie all rushed down the path together. Then Zoe's mom arrived with some of the other zookeepers, looking very out of breath. "The zoo visitors must be wondering what's going on!" She laughed, hugging Great-Uncle Horace. "The animals are making a lot of noise, and all the zoo staff are dashing down the path as if they're running a race!"

"This is impossible," spluttered a voice from behind them. "*Two* new pandas? That's twice the money. *And* twice the mess!"

Zoe turned, her heart sinking. Mr.

Pinch, the zoo manager, was standing by the gate, his skinny arms folded tightly. His uniform was crisply ironed and his shoes perfectly polished, but his thin face was as sour as vinegar.

Only horrible Mr. Pinch could be grumpy about such beautiful creatures arriving at the zoo! thought Zoe.

"Ah, Mr. Pinch! A pleasure as always," Great-Uncle Horace called, his eyes twinkling. "I see you've come to meet our new arrivals."

"Mr. Higgins, *delightful* to have you back, of course," Mr. Pinch added quickly, his cheeks flushing pink. "But perhaps we should discuss this before we do anything *hasty*. I really do not see how the pandas can stay here. One cub would be very expensive, but *two*—"

"Yes, two!" Great-Uncle Horace interrupted cheerfully. "Two pandas, who *both* need a home. Remember, the Rescue Zoo never turns an animal away—no matter what."

Mr. Pinch went the color of a ripe tomato. "Well, no," he snapped. "But the cost—"

"We'll think of something!" Great-Uncle Horace told him, walking over to the flustered zoo manager and patting his shoulder. "Let's go to my office for a chat. I know you must have some excellent ideas up your sleeve! Besides, it's time I had a cup of tea and a cookie. Come along, Kiki. See you later, everyone." He marched away down the path with Kiki soaring above him. Mr. Pinch shot the pandas a final angry look and then followed, grumbling under his breath.

Stephanie jumped to her feet. "Right, everyone! Let's get this enclosure fixed up for the cubs."

The zookeepers set to work. Frankie collected some fresh wood chippings for the ground, while Jess found a pile of warm, fleecy blankets for the cubs to sleep on. Everyone else swept away the piles of autumn leaves and cut the sprawling ivy off the wooden platforms.

Meanwhile, Zoe's mom checked the cubs to make sure they were both healthy.

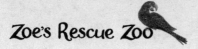

As Zoe held each cub carefully in her
lap, her mom used the stethoscope around
her neck to listen to their heartbeats.

Then she opened the special vet bag
she always carried and shone a small
flashlight into their eyes and ears. "They're
both perfect," she told Zoe, smiling. "This
one here is a little bit bigger than her
sister, but that happens quite often when
two babies are born at the same time."

Soon there was only one job left. "We need to fix the wooden fence around the enclosure," said Stephanie. "Some of the wood has rotted away, and the bamboo has grown so much that it's pushed holes right through it!"

Will and Jess fetched new pieces of wood and some nails from the zoo storehouse, and used them to patch up the holes in the fence.

Finally all the work was done, and the twins' enclosure looked as good as new. "Thanks for your help, everyone!" called Stephanie as the keepers left in small groups, chatting about the adorable cubs.

Zoe's mom gave Zoe a kiss before heading back to the zoo hospital. "I have to check on a sick raccoon, and give some medicine to an aardvark with a sore

snout," she said. "I expect you and Meep
will be here all day! Just be home in time
for dinner."

As Zoe's mom set off down the path,
Stephanie grinned at Zoe. "I think it's
lunchtime for hungry panda cubs!" she
announced. "I'll fetch some milk. Will you
watch them until I'm back?"

"Of course!" said Zoe quickly. She
caught Meep's eye and the little lemur
chirped excitedly. Being alone with
the cubs meant she'd be able to talk to
them—with no one else around this time!
As soon as Stephanie left the enclosure,
Zoe knelt down. The bigger cub was
playing happily with a twig while her
sister was quietly watching a worm
wriggle along the ground.

"Hello!" she said softly. "I'm Zoe and

this is my best friend, Meep. What are your names?"

The bigger cub looked up and squeaked in surprise. Zoe giggled. "Yes, that's right—I *can* talk to animals. You weren't imagining it! I wasn't supposed to do it before though. I forgot my great-uncle was here."

The cub squeaked again, eagerly. "Chi Chi," Zoe said, nodding. "That's such a pretty name. What about you, little one?"

The smaller cub blinked at her, then squealed shyly. "Mei Mei," repeated Zoe, smiling gently at her. "We're so pleased you've come to the Rescue Zoo. We're going to look after you here, I promise."

Meep chattered a warning as Stephanie came back into the enclosure. "Zoe, do you want to feed one of the cubs?" she asked, holding up two bottles of warm milk. "I know you're an expert!"

Zoe grinned happily. "Yes, *please*!" she said, taking a bottle from Stephanie. She loved feeding baby animals!

Carefully, she picked up Mei Mei and held the little panda against her chest. With a tiny squeak, Mei Mei cuddled up against Zoe. Her fur was so soft and fluffy, and she felt very warm. Zoe offered her the bottle and Mei Mei started drinking the milk happily.

Stephanie smiled as she fed Chi Chi. "We're so lucky to have them here, you know," she told Zoe. "Pandas are some of the most vulnerable animals in the world. There are fewer than two thousand living in the wild now."

Zoe frowned. She knew that sounded like a big number, but it was actually very low. There were almost a thousand people in her school, and that was the same as half of all the pandas living wild in the whole wide world. "Why aren't there more?" she asked.

"There are lots of reasons," Stephanie explained. "Poachers hunt pandas because they can sell their fur for lots of money. Pandas need to eat so much bamboo that it's really hard for them to find homes with enough plants growing nearby. Plus, pandas don't have babies very often—and twins are especially unusual."

Chi Chi finished her milk and gave a little hiccup. Stephanie laughed. "They certainly enjoyed that!" she said, tickling the cub's fluffy belly.

"I've thought of some names, Stephanie," said Zoe. "What about Chi Chi for that cub, and Mei Mei for this one?"

"Those are perfect!" Stephanie exclaimed. "In Chinese, 'Mei Mei' means 'little sister.' How did you know that?"

Zoe thought quickly. "I . . . I learned it at school," she explained, hoping she wasn't blushing. Zoe didn't like making up stories, but sometimes it was the only way to cover up her secret. She couldn't tell Stephanie that the baby pandas had told her their names!

When Mei Mei had finished her bottle, Zoe and Stephanie put both pandas down. Right away, Chi Chi was ready to explore. She scampered over to the nearest wooden platform and climbed up the ramp, with a little help from Stephanie. At the top, she squeaked happily, excited to see her new home from high up. Then she padded back down the ramp and dashed over to the waterfall. "You're going to be a little handful, Chi Chi. I can tell already!" Stephanie laughed, chasing after her.

Zoe glanced down curiously at Mei Mei, who had crept onto her lap. The smaller panda watched her sister quietly but didn't seem to want to join in. "Don't you want to explore, Mei Mei?" Zoe whispered, but the cub shook her head.

A moment later Chi Chi came charging back through the enclosure and nudged her little sister with her front paws, squeaking bossily. Mei Mei cuddled closer to Zoe and whimpered. Stephanie scratched her head. "It's funny that they're not playing together," she said, puzzled. "They must have been cooped up together for too long. They just need a little bit of space and they'll be rolling around together soon enough."

But Zoe and Meep looked at each other in alarm. They had understood Chi Chi and Mei Mei's panda noises and knew what was wrong. Chi Chi thought her sister was a baby because she didn't want to explore and play. Mei Mei didn't want to do the scary things Chi Chi did and thought her sister was a show-off.

Oh no! The panda twins didn't seem to like each other at all!

Chapter Five
Squabbling Sisters

As Zoe got ready for bed that evening
she couldn't stop worrying about the
little pandas. All afternoon the sisters had
squabbled. Zoe had encouraged them to
play together, but energetic Chi Chi had
just squeaked angrily at quiet Mei Mei,
who was still feeling nervous in her new
home. Stephanie had been disappointed,

and even Great-Uncle Horace had
looked concerned when he came by the
cottage to say good-night. "We'll try
again tomorrow," he'd said reassuringly.
"Perhaps the twins are tired after traveling
such a long way."

Zoe brushed her teeth, put on her
orange tiger-striped pajamas, and climbed
into bed. Meep was already curled up
on her pillow. The little lemur looked
worried too. Zoe switched off the dolphin
lamp next to her bed and sighed. "What
are we going to do, Meep? Great-Uncle
Horace brought the sisters to the Rescue
Zoo so they could stay together, but they
just don't get along."

"But *why*, Zoe?" Meep asked, his little
nose wrinkled up anxiously. "I don't
understand."

"I think it's because they're so different," Zoe said thoughtfully. "Chi Chi is playful and adventurous, while Mei Mei's timid and quiet. They're so lucky though," she added. "I'd *love* to have a sister or a brother, even if we were really different! Someone I could always play with, and tell all my problems and secrets."

"But you have me, Zoe!" Meep chattered happily, snuggling up against her. "We play together a lot. *And* I already know your biggest secret!"

Zoe laughed and pulled Meep close for a cuddle. "That's true, Meep. I don't need anyone else when I've got you!" She rubbed her cheek against his furry head. "But the pandas *do* need each other. Tomorrow we have to find a way to help them get along!"

The next morning Zoe ran out of the cottage as soon as she'd eaten a quick bowl of oatmeal and Meep had munched a banana. Zoe was desperate to get to the panda enclosure early, before the visitors started arriving.

"Maybe the pandas will be playing together when we get there," Meep chirped brightly as they dashed down the path. Zoe hoped her little friend was right.

As they stepped into the enclosure, Zoe saw Mei Mei padding curiously up to the waterfall. "Look, Meep!" Zoe whispered. "She's finally feeling brave enough to explore!"

Then Chi Chi noticed what her sister was doing. With a happy squeal, Chi Chi scrambled toward Mei Mei and bumped playfully into her. Poor Mei Mei wobbled . . . and fell underneath the waterfall with a big splash! "Naughty Chi Chi," Zoe muttered as the older cub scampered quickly away, and Mei Mei gave a cross squeak. "That's no way to make friends."

Stephanie had just arrived at the enclosure. "Morning, Zoe," she called.

"Could you grab a blanket from the pandas' sleeping area? We'll need to dry Mei Mei. I'm afraid the cubs still aren't getting along."

Zoe fetched a fluffy blanket as a very wet Mei Mei waddled over. She scooped the panda up and rubbed her fur gently with the blanket. "There, you're nice and dry," she soothed, making sure she spoke too quietly for Stephanie to hear. "Chi Chi was just playing."

Stephanie sighed. "It's such a shame. Both cubs seem to love their new home. Chi Chi adores the wooden platforms and the ramps, and even Mei Mei's starting to settle in. But if they don't make friends soon . . ." She hesitated.

"Then what will happen?" Zoe asked immediately.

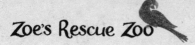

"We'll have to split them up," Stephanie explained. "While they're little they can't do any harm, but when they're fully grown they might hurt each other."

"But we'd be able to keep them both at the zoo, wouldn't we?" Zoe asked anxiously. "One could stay here and the other could go in a different enclosure."

Stephanie shook her head sadly. "I'm afraid not, sweetheart. We don't have any spare enclosures big enough for an adult panda. They need *lots* of space, you see. One sister would probably have to go to another zoo."

Zoe's heart sank. It was horrible to imagine the sisters not liking each other, and it was even worse to think about them being separated. What if one of the twins was sent back to China? That was thousands of miles away. They would never see each other again.

Suddenly Zoe remembered something. *Su Lin*. Her old friend had loved telling stories about her little sister and all the fun they'd had together. Su Lin and Bai Yun had been separated when they were still very young. But Su Lin had *never* stopped missing Bai Yun, even years later. Zoe took a deep, determined breath. She was *not* going to let that happen to Chi Chi and Mei Mei. She had to make them see how lucky they were to have each other.

Stephanie gave her hand a gentle squeeze. "I'm sorry, Zoe. I didn't mean to worry you," she said. "Listen, cheer up. It's breakfast time and we're going to try giving the cubs some solid food today."

She had brought a small plastic box with her that morning, and now she took the lid off. It was full of apples and bamboo, sliced up into tiny chunks. "It might seem silly to bring bamboo when there's so much growing around us," she said. "But until the babies' teeth grow stronger, it's very hard for them to bite into. I cut up the softest, freshest piece I could find, to make it easier for them."

She gave the box a little shake. Chi Chi's black nose twitched and she scampered toward them, excited by the smell of the juicy bamboo. Mei Mei looked curious and followed cautiously.

Stephanie glanced down at her watch. "Oh dear. I've just remembered—I'm supposed to be over at Alex's enclosure in five minutes. He hasn't had his breakfast bananas yet, and you know how grumpy the old gorilla gets when he's hungry!"

"I can feed the pandas!" Zoe offered quickly, winking at Meep. The little lemur chirped. They both knew the more time they could spend alone with the cubs, the better chance they had of helping them become friends with each other.

Stephanie beamed at her. "Are you sure? Zoe, you're amazing. I'll be back really soon."

Stephanie handed the plastic box to Zoe and dashed out of the enclosure. When she was out of sight, Zoe glanced around, making sure no one else was on the path nearby. Then she crouched down and tipped a few slices of bamboo into her palm. "Come on, you two!" she said softly. "Are you hungry?"

Both cubs nodded their heads eagerly. Zoe smiled. "I have lots of tasty treats for you," she told them. "But this bamboo is *only* for pandas who behave nicely."

The cubs blinked innocently up at her. *I hope that worked!* thought Zoe. Carefully, she handed one piece of bamboo to each twin. They both grasped the pieces in their paws, sniffed at them, and then started to nibble. A moment later

Chi Chi squeaked happily, and Mei Mei's dark eyes went wide with delight.

Zoe giggled. This was the first time the pandas had ever tried bamboo—and they loved it! And for the first time that morning they weren't fighting.

But it didn't last very long. As soon as naughty Chi Chi finished her bamboo, she reached over and grabbed Mei Mei's piece out of her paws and gobbled it up! Mei Mei turned to Zoe and wailed.

"No, that *wasn't* very fair of Chi Chi," admitted Zoe. "But it's all right, there's a lot more bamboo for you both."

But the older panda was just as mad now! Chi Chi thumped her little paw on the ground and squeaked indignantly.

"Chi Chi! Calling your sister a tattletale isn't very nice," scolded Zoe, feeling more and more worried. "Come on, there's no need to argue. Why don't you try a piece of apple this time?"

But the cubs had forgotten all about their treats, and suddenly Zoe couldn't get a word in over their angry squabbling. Her heart sank even further as Chi Chi pushed her sister. The playful panda was very naughty!

Meep chirped a sudden warning and from behind her Zoe heard a loud, sneering voice. "Fussing and fighting already, I see. I just *knew* those pandas would be trouble."

Zoe groaned quietly as horrible Mr. Pinch marched into the enclosure. This morning was getting worse and worse!

Chapter Six
Double Trouble

Mr. Pinch peered snootily around the enclosure. "I was expecting to find a real, *grown-up* zookeeper here," he announced, narrowing his eyes at Zoe.

Meep leaped onto Zoe's shoulder and chattered angrily, and Zoe shot her little friend a warning look. Mr. Pinch did not approve of Zoe and Meep wandering freely around the zoo and all the enclosures. Even when they were trying to help, he would grumble, "Miss Parker, this is a job for *zoo staff*—not a little girl and a naughty lemur!"

"Stephanie went to give Alex his breakfast," Zoe told Mr. Pinch politely. "I promised to stay and watch the cubs while she was gone."

Just then Chi Chi let out an especially noisy squeal and thumped Mei Mei with her little paw. Mr. Pinch glared down his long thin nose at the bickering pandas. "I've heard all about the pandas fighting," he announced. "I *told* Mr. Higgins they would be a nuisance! But they won't be causing trouble in my zoo for long." He nodded his head bossily. "Mr. Higgins wants there to be a special event on

Friday to welcome the pandas to the
Rescue Zoo. Lots of important people
will be there: visitors, news reporters,
even the mayor! I won't have the cubs
acting up in front of them. If they are still
fighting by then, I'll start proceedings to
send one of them to another zoo."

Meep gave a squeak of alarm, and Zoe
stared at Mr. Pinch in horror. "But—
but Friday is just a few days away!" she
stammered, glancing at the squabbling
cubs. It seemed almost impossible that
they would be friends by then.

"Well, they'd better start getting along
quickly!" Mr. Pinch told her nastily. "Now,
I've come to take some photos of the cubs
so I can make posters for the event. I'd
better get started. I'm *very* busy, as usual."
He pulled a camera out of his pocket and

pointed at Chi Chi. "That one first."

He stepped over to the little panda. But as he held the camera up to his face, Chi Chi rolled away from him with a playful squeal.

"Sit still!" Mr. Pinch snapped.

He moved toward Chi Chi again. But the cub gave another excited squeak and scampered quickly around Mr. Pinch, so that she was perched behind him. Mr. Pinch whirled around angrily—and playful Chi Chi turned a somersault through his legs, landing right back where she'd started!

"That's enough!" Mr. Pinch spluttered, suddenly looking very hot and red. "I will *not* stand for such rude behavior. I am the *zoo manager*! Well, if *you* won't behave, I'll take a photo of your sister first."

He turned to Mei Mei, who gazed up at him quietly. Next to bold, naughty Chi Chi she looked so timid and well-behaved, so what happened next was even more of a surprise. The little panda poked her tiny pink tongue out at Mr. Pinch!

Chi Chi let out a delighted squeak of laughter at her sister being naughty. She scrambled over to Mei Mei and playfully rolled her around on the ground, squealing happily. When they sat up again, they were covered in dirt, mud, and twig. Mr. Pinch stared angrily at them. "Naughty, messy creatures," he fumed. "I can't tell them apart now!"

Zoe looked at the cubs. *She* knew which fluffy bundle was Chi Chi and which was Mei Mei—even though the splotch on Mei Mei's tummy was hidden by

the mud! But something was different about them. The cubs were huddled close, whispering to each other. Their eyes were bright and excited. *They're having fun together,* Zoe realized, suddenly feeling hopeful. *They're really getting along. And it's because they both love causing trouble for Mr. Pinch!*

The zoo manager scowled at her, his

face very pink. "Which one is which?" he snapped. "I don't have all day."

"That's Chi Chi," Zoe said, pointing. "She's the older twin. And that's Mei Mei. She's a tiny bit smaller than her sister."

"Well, they're both just as troublesome as each other, if you ask me," Mr. Pinch grumbled. "Now, where's my camera? I dropped it over here somewhere."

He turned around to pick up the camera, muttering angrily. While he was looking away, Mei Mei leaned over to squeak in her sister's ear. Chi Chi giggled . . . and just before Mr. Pinch turned back, the twins swapped places!

Meep squealed with laughter and Zoe couldn't help smiling. The silly pandas were just too funny, and she was so relieved to see them starting to become friends. Mr. Pinch narrowed his eyes at her suspiciously. "You'd better not be tricking me," he warned her. "If you are, you'll be in big trouble!"

"I'm not tricking you, I promise," Zoe said truthfully. *After all,* she thought, *I did tell you the truth. It wasn't my fault the babies switched!*

Mr. Pinch scowled at the muddy pandas. "Now the little pests are going to be all dirty on my posters," he grumbled.

He held up the camera again. Right away, the cubs took off! Chi Chi scampered playfully in one direction, toward the waterfall. Mei Mei padded the other way, past the wooden platforms.

"Come back here this instant!" Mr. Pinch shouted. But the cubs tumbled from one part of the enclosure to another and

never stayed still long enough for the furious zoo manager to take their photos.

Mr. Pinch chased them until he was gasping for breath. Eventually he threw his hands in the air. His hat was tipped crookedly over one eye and his face was red and hot. "I give up!" he snapped. "Never, in all my years as manager of the Rescue Zoo, have I seen such naughty behavior. I'll be informing Mr. Higgins about this."

He stormed out of the enclosure and down the path, muttering fiercely under his breath. As soon as he turned the corner, Zoe and Meep looked at each other and giggled. "That was so much fun," the little lemur chattered gleefully. "Horrid old Pinch was as red as a raspberry!"

Zoe grinned happily. Together the twins were double trouble! But she didn't mind. All that mattered was that the sisters were starting to get along, and as long as they were friends they could *both* stay at the Rescue Zoo. She just hoped it would last.

"Chi Chi! Mei Mei!" she called. "He's gone! Come and finish your breakfast now."

The pandas bounded back over, and she bent down to give them both a hug. Chi Chi squeaked brightly up at her. Zoe laughed. "Yes, it looked like you were enjoying yourself!" she told the silly little cub.

She handed out the rest of the apple and bamboo and held her breath, hoping the cubs would nibble their treats happily this time. But her heart sank as naughty

Chi Chi snatched her sister's apple and scrambled playfully away with it, while Mei Mei gave a cross little squeak. Chi Chi grumbled that Mei Mei was no fun— and suddenly the pandas were fighting all over again.

"They're still not getting along, Meep." Zoe groaned. "I can't believe it. I thought they were starting to become friends, but that was only when they were having fun teasing Mr. Pinch. Now that he's gone, they're arguing just like before." She glanced at the older cub, who was splashing around in the waterfall. "Chi Chi just wants to play and be naughty. She doesn't understand that Mei Mei is quieter and doesn't always want to join in."

Meep's little nose wrinkled up anxiously. "What should we do, Zoe?" he chirped.

Zoe bit her lip, feeling very worried. "We'd better go and find Stephanie and tell her what Mr. Pinch said. This is really serious. If the babies don't become friends before Friday, one of them will be sent away. We can't let that happen!"

Chapter Seven
Missing Mei Mei

On Friday, Zoe flew into the cottage and dropped her schoolbag on the kitchen table. "Meep!" she called breathlessly. "I'm back. I ran all the way home!"

There was a tiny squeak from the bowl of bananas on the counter. Then Meep's furry little head popped up, munching away. "Meep, you're supposed to *peel* the

83

bananas
before you
eat them!"
Zoe told
her friend,
gathering
him up for a
hug. "Come on,
let's go straight to
the panda enclosure.
Today's the special welcome event! A lot
of important people will be arriving soon,
all wanting to meet Chi Chi and Mei
Mei—and Mr. Pinch will be watching to
see if they're getting along."

Meep's golden eyes were wide with
worry. "I peeked into their enclosure at
lunchtime, Zoe. They were still fighting!"
the little lemur told her.

Zoe sighed. "They haven't stopped fighting all week, Meep. I think this is our last chance to make them become friends."

She ran up to her bedroom and quickly swapped her school uniform for jeans and a warm red sweater, and pushed a ball into her backpack. Otto and Benedict had loved playing with a ball; maybe Chi Chi and Mei Mei would too? As they set off into the zoo, Zoe sighed. Every day that week, as soon as she'd arrived home from school, she and Meep had raced to visit Chi Chi and Mei Mei. They had tried everything they could think of to make the cubs get along, but nothing seemed to work.

Once, Stephanie had let Zoe bring an old tire into the enclosure for the sisters to play with. Chi Chi had loved it, but Mei Mei gave a frightened squeak whenever it rolled near her and Chi Chi had called her a baby. Another time Zoe had suggested they try a quiet game of sleeping logs. Mei Mei's eyes had lit up, but Chi Chi snorted that it sounded boring. Yesterday Zoe had tried explaining how important it was that they become friends, but Mei Mei didn't seem to understand and Chi Chi was too busy rolling in the mud to listen. Zoe hoped the ball worked—she wasn't sure what else to try.

The only time the twins had fun together was when Mr. Pinch came to their enclosure. He had tried to take photos of them for his posters every day that week, and became angrier and angrier each time. As soon as he appeared, the twins would whisper mischievously and hide from him until he stomped away. In the end, Mr. Pinch had to make do with some blurry pictures of Chi Chi's paw and Mei Mei's ear, which he was very grumpy about.

It was a sunny afternoon, and the zoo was full of visitors enjoying themselves. As Zoe and Meep reached the panda enclosure, a crowd of little girls was gathered outside, one of them holding a birthday balloon and wearing a sparkly badge. "Look at the little panda—he's so cute!" she told her friends. "But I thought there were two? Mommy told me there were twin pandas."

"I can only see one," another girl agreed, standing on tiptoe to have a better look.

Zoe glanced over the fence. Chi Chi was huddled by herself in front of a big clump of bamboo next to the fence at the edge of the enclosure. "Mei Mei must be hiding from Mr. Pinch again," she whispered to Meep. "But why does Chi Chi look so sad? That's not like her."

The group of girls took some pictures of themselves standing next to the fence, with Chi Chi in the background. As they rushed off to visit the hippos, Zoe pulled out her paw-print charm and opened the gate. "Chi Chi, it's us!" she called softly as they stepped inside. "Is everything all right? Where's Mei Mei?"

When she heard Zoe's voice, Chi Chi looked up and let out a miserable whimper. Zoe and Meep hurried over to the little panda, and Zoe knelt down beside her. "What do you mean, Mei Mei's gone?" she asked. "Where?"

Chi Chi sniffled sadly and crept behind the big clump of bamboo. Zoe peered after her and gasped. The bamboo was covering a big hole in the fence—a hole that the zookeepers hadn't patched up. And Mei Mei had disappeared through it!

Chapter Eight
Panda Panic

Zoe gazed in horror at the hole. "I don't understand, Chi Chi," she said, panic spreading through her tummy. "Mei Mei's so shy. Why did she escape?"

Chi Chi gulped and gave a little squeak. Zoe listened carefully as the little cub explained what had happened. When timid Mei Mei had found the hole in the fence, she'd decided to prove to her sister that she *wasn't* a baby. She was going to squeeze through it and explore the rest of the zoo! But bold, brave Chi Chi had been too frightened to follow.

Meep scampered over to the baby panda and gave her a comforting hug, while Zoe stroked her soft little head. "It's all right," she told her, trying not to let Chi Chi see how worried she was. "Mei Mei can't have gone very far. We'll find her, I promise."

Suddenly she heard a familiar, bossy voice coming down the path. "This way, this way! Follow me, everyone!" Mr. Pinch called loudly. "The pandas are just around this corner."

Quickly, Zoe and Meep squeezed behind the bamboo with Chi Chi, so that they couldn't be seen from the path. A huge chattering crowd of people was gathering outside the enclosure to meet the pandas. A lot of them were wearing important-looking badges, and some of them carried microphones or big TV cameras. Stephanie was there too, peering anxiously over the fence to see if the pandas were fighting or not.

"So where are they?" asked a reporter with big square glasses and a green tie. "I can't see either of them!"

"They're probably just having a little snooze somewhere," explained Stephanie. "Baby pandas as young as Chi Chi and Mei Mei need lots of sleep."

"Ahem! Yes, well, *I* knew that, of course," Mr. Pinch interrupted pompously.

Zoe's mind was racing. She had to act fast, before Mr. Pinch decided to come into the enclosure and start looking for the cubs. "Meep, we've got to find Mei Mei. She's small and, with such a big crowd of people here, she must be frightened," she whispered to the little lemur.

"Maybe we should ask all those people to look for her too?" Meep suggested.

Zoe shook her head. "We can't let anyone know Mei Mei's not in her enclosure. If the reporters find out a rare

baby panda has managed to escape, it
would be a disaster for the Rescue Zoo!"

She turned to Chi Chi. "Stay here, and
we'll go search for Mei Mei."

But the little panda shook her head
stubbornly and squeaked. Zoe hesitated.
"You can't come with me, Chi Chi. What
if someone saw you?"

Chi Chi squeaked again and nudged her little nose against Zoe's backpack. Zoe couldn't help smiling. "OK—as long as you promise to stay very quiet and don't pop your head out. And no tickling me!"

Zoe emptied out the backpack and let Chi Chi wriggle inside. Taking a deep breath, she crept toward the gate, trying to stay hidden behind trees and huge bamboo plants so that the crowd wouldn't notice her. "It's lucky the enclosure is still so wild and overgrown!" she whispered to Meep.

Suddenly one of the reporters shouted, "I think I can see them! Over there, by that wooden platform!"

While the crowd was distracted, Zoe slipped out the gate and back onto the path.

Just as she was about to start searching, someone tapped her on the shoulder.

"Zoe!" said a relieved voice. "Just the person I was hoping to see. How was school today?"

Zoe whirled around. "Mom!" she stammered, desperately hoping her mom wouldn't ask what was in her backpack, or see it wriggling. "Er—school was fine."

"Listen, Zoe, I need you to help me," her mom said. "I was on my way to the gazelle enclosure with some medicine for Gordon's sick tummy, but I've just had an urgent call on my walkie-talkie. One of the brown bear cubs has a thorn stuck in his paw, and I need to take him to the zoo hospital. The poor little thing's very upset! Could you take the medicine to Gordon?" She pulled a small bottle from the special vet bag she always carried and passed it to Zoe.

Zoe's heart sank, but she nodded. As her mom hurried off, Zoe whispered urgently to Meep, "Start telling all the animals about the missing cub. Ask them to help spread the word! Oscar can sound the alarm with his giant trunk, and the birds can fly around and search from the sky. We'll meet back here in five minutes. There's no time to lose!"

Chapter Nine
The Search Is On

Zoe didn't think she'd ever run so fast.
Clutching the medicine in one hand,
she raced through the zoo, dodging and
weaving past visitors. She could feel the
backpack bumping against her back as
she sped along and hoped she wasn't
making Chi Chi dizzy. "Excuse me!" she
panted breathlessly. "Animal emergency!"

Her heart was thumping hard in her chest when she reached the grassy plain next to the lake, where the gazelles grazed. "Ah, Zoe!" called the gazelle-keeper, waving. "Your mom said you'd be bringing—"

"Really sorry!" Zoe gasped, flinging the bottle into his hands and sprinting off again. "Can't stop now!"

Zoe raced around the zoo, calling out to the animals. The news of the escaped cub was spreading quickly. The zebras stamped their hooves and whinnied the message to their neighbors, the alpine hares. The flamingos flapped their wings and hooted to the wolves, who howled so loudly that every animal in the zoo could hear them. The warthogs snuffled around in their cool mud holes to make

sure Mei Mei wasn't there. The baboons checked in the bushes, and one of the crocodiles politely asked Zoe what the missing panda looked like. Zoe unzipped her backpack so Chi Chi could peep out. "Exactly like this!" she replied, holding the little cub up in the air. But it was no good, no one had seen Mei Mei.

They were almost back at the panda enclosure when Meep came scampering around the corner to meet them. "Everyone's looking for Mei Mei, but there's no sign of her anywhere," he chattered. "What shall we do next?"

Zoe bit her lip and thought. "Let's go back to the enclosure again," she suggested. "We'll look for paw prints near the hole in the fence or any other clue that might lead us to Mei Mei."

Chi Chi squeaked eagerly in agreement.
Zoe zipped up her backpack, and they
crept along to the panda enclosure. There
was a grumble of voices as they arrived.
The crowd was getting restless and cranky.
Zoe saw the reporter with the glasses
check his watch and shake his head.
"How long do we have to wait to see
these pandas?" he complained.

Suddenly a blur of deep-blue feathers
swooped past his head, making him
jump. Kiki landed on top of the fence
and fluttered her wings as Great-Uncle
Horace strolled down the path, crunching
on a cookie. "Good afternoon, everyone!"
he called cheerily, tipping his explorer's
hat to the crowd. "It's wonderful that
you've all come to meet our special new
arrivals!"

One of the reporters sighed loudly. "Well, we haven't met them yet," he complained. "We haven't even caught a glimpse of them. I'm going home if they don't show up soon!"

"Oh, what a pity," Great-Uncle Horace said with concern. "You really must wait and see them. Pandas are so rare, especially twins." He smiled brightly at the man. "Did you know that in China they are called 'giant bear cats'? Some people also call them 'bamboo bears.' Fascinating!"

The crowd gathered around Great-Uncle Horace as he began telling them all about pandas. Even the grumpy reporter looked interested. Zoe knew he'd only be distracted for a few minutes though. She had to find Mei Mei and get both cubs back into their home—fast!

Quietly, she tiptoed around the outside of the enclosure until she found where the hole in the fence was hidden. Chi Chi started wriggling so much in the backpack that Zoe let her out. Together, Zoe, Meep, and Chi Chi all began looking for any sign of Mei Mei. Then Chi Chi squealed eagerly.

"What have you found, Chi Chi?" chirped Meep, hopping up and down.

Chi Chi lifted her paw and pointed. A wisp of white fluff was caught on the branch of a tall oak tree, just outside the enclosure. With an excited squeak, Chi Chi scampered up the tree.

"Chi Chi!" Zoe called in a loud whisper. It was just like naughty Chi Chi to run off when they needed her!

The little panda disappeared up the tree trunk and was soon invisible among the branches. Zoe sighed. Instead of finding one panda, now she'd lost two!

"Chi Chi!" she whispered again.

Suddenly there was a suspicious voice behind her. "Just what do you think you are doing, Miss Parker?"

Chapter Ten
Friends Forever

"Mr. Pinch!" Zoe stammered, feeling her cheeks flush pink. Carefully, she stepped to one side so that the zoo manager couldn't see the hole in the fence. "I was just . . . er . . . looking for the pandas." She peered into the enclosure. "I thought I might be able to see them from this side of the enclosure, but I, um, can't."

The grumpy zoo manager glared at her. "Well, I'm looking for them myself," he told her bossily. "The crowd is fed up waiting, and I won't let those two little pests spoil the special event! They have to be around here somewhere." He peered into the enclosure and added angrily, "There are just so many of these big clumps of bamboo that they could have hidden behind!"

Zoe glanced up at the tree. Chi Chi's black-and-white face peered out from the branches. Then next to her there was a flash of black and white, and another face appeared. There wasn't just one baby panda in the tree, but two! Chi Chi had found Mei Mei!

Zoe had to hide her grin as Mr. Pinch looked at her curiously.

There was another rustling sound from inside the tree, and a high, happy squeaking sound. Mr. Pinch looked around, puzzled. "Can you hear that? There's definitely a panda close by!" he muttered.

Zoe looked at Meep desperately. "We can't let Mr. Pinch see that the cubs are out of their enclosure!" she whispered. "Can you distract him?"

Meep's little face lit up. "I can be just as playful as Chi Chi!" he told her proudly.

With a nimble leap, he sprang over to the zoo manager. It had rained that morning and there was a muddy puddle next to him. With a gleeful chirp, Meep jumped into it, splashing mud on the zoo manager's shiny shoes.

Mr. Pinch stared down at the mess in disbelief. "I polished my shoes this morning!" he spluttered. "You little nuisance! I'll have to clean these before the reporters see." He shook his head angrily and pointed a finger at Zoe. "If those pesky pandas haven't appeared by the time I'm back, I'm going into the enclosure to search every inch until I find them!"

As Mr. Pinch stomped off down the path, Zoe turned to the tree. "Chi Chi?" she called softly. "You can come down now. He's gone!"

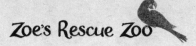

There was a giggle, and Chi Chi slid down the tree trunk, her eyes bright. Then the branches shook gently again— and another face popped out of the leaves, squeaking happily.

"Mei Mei!" cried Zoe. "I'm so happy to see you!"

"Hooray!" cried Meep, bouncing up and down.

Both pandas scrambled down from the tree. Zoe laughed as they leaped into her arms and they all shared a fluffy hug. "I'm so glad you're all right, Mei Mei," she told the little panda. "We were all so worried about you!"

Chi Chi nuzzled Mei Mei with her black nose, squealing eagerly. "Mei Mei *was* very brave to go exploring all by herself, Chi Chi," Zoe agreed, smiling.

"And she *did* find the best hiding place yet from Mr. Pinch! But I think you'd both better stay *inside* your home from now on, don't you?"

Mei Mei nodded, and Zoe grinned as the cubs squeaked and chattered in delight about their adventure. While they were apart, they had realized how much they missed each other. Now they were so happy to be back together, safe and sound.

Suddenly Meep tugged on Zoe's sleeve with his tiny fingers. "Quick, Zoe," he chirped. "Mr. Pinch is back!"

Zoe placed the cubs carefully on the ground, and they squeezed back through the hole in the fence and peeked out from behind the bamboo. The zoo manager was inside the enclosure, looking out at the grumbling crowd. "They must be in here somewhere," he announced, trying to sound cheerful.

"I've had enough of this," snapped one of the reporters. "I don't believe there really *are* any pandas in there. I think you've been making it all up!"

As Mr. Pinch spluttered, Meep turned to Zoe. "If all those people leave without seeing the pandas, they'll be very angry," the little lemur chattered nervously. "They might even tell people not to come to the Rescue Zoo anymore!"

"There's something even more important to think about, Meep," Zoe replied. "If Mr. Pinch doesn't see that the pandas are getting along now, he might

still decide to send one of them away.
Remember, he said they had to be friends
by today!"

She looked through the wire enclosure
and laughed. "But I don't think we need
to worry about that anymore, Meep,"
she giggled happily.

Side by side, Chi Chi and Mei Mei
scampered out from behind the bamboo
and padded toward the crowd. As they
got closer, Mei Mei leaped playfully onto
her sister and they rolled around in a pile
of leaves, giggling and squealing. Chi Chi
was proud of her brave sister. Even better,
Mei Mei was no longer too timid and
frightened to try new things. In fact, Mei
Mei seemed just as bold and brave as Chi
Chi—rolling, scampering, and having fun
in her home more than ever before.

"After their big adventure, the cubs have realized how much they love each other!" Zoe grinned as she listened to their excited squeals. "They've become friends for good this time."

Suddenly the reporters spotted them,

and there were gasps and laughs from the crowd. "Look—there they are!" one cried. "I don't believe it. They're even cuter than I imagined!"

"And look at them playing together. They're beautiful," added another, taking a picture.

Mr. Pinch stared at the pandas, completely baffled. "Where on earth were the little fluffballs hiding?" he muttered. "I looked *everywhere!*"

While the crowd was busy watching the pandas, Zoe covered up the hole in the fence with an armful of dry sticks and twigs. "We'll make sure Stephanie fixes it later," she whispered to Meep. "But something tells me the cubs won't be trying to escape again anytime soon!"

Quietly, they slipped back to the gate and out onto the path. Zoe ran up behind Stephanie and Great-Uncle Horace, and tapped them both on the shoulder.

"There you are, sweetheart!" Stephanie cried, throwing her arms around Zoe.

"I was wondering where you were. Quick, take a look at Chi Chi and Mei Mei! I don't know what happened, but suddenly they're getting along so well!"

"It's extraordinary," added Great-Uncle Horace, his brown eyes twinkling at Zoe. "And just in time!"

The gate opened again and out came Mr. Pinch. Zoe waited for him to storm and shout about the naughty cubs, but the zoo manager was delighted. "The reporters say they'll tell all their friends to come to the zoo to see the pandas," he announced smugly. "One of them even promised to write a special story about how rare they are. You don't see twin pandas every day, after all. That means extra visitors for the Rescue Zoo—and extra money! It was a great idea of mine, making sure we kept them both." He strolled off down the path, whistling a happy tune.

"Will the sisters always be together, Mr. Higgins?" called a reporter, holding a microphone out to Great-Uncle Horace.

"Always," he replied, beaming at Zoe. "The cubs are not just sisters. They are also the very best of friends. We would never dream of separating them."

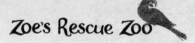

Zoe beamed back at Great-Uncle Horace and turned to watch the baby pandas rolling around together. She was so relieved and so happy! The twins were both going to stay at the Rescue Zoo and enjoy being together.

Just then Mei Mei leaped into the waterfall, splashing Chi Chi.

The crowd chuckled and Meep giggled so hard he fell over! Zoe grinned and scooped her little friend into her arms for a hug. "It looks like the Rescue Zoo doesn't have just one playful panda anymore, Meep," she whispered happily. "Now we have two!"

Read about Zoe's first animal adventure!

The cub blinked nervously at the crowd. He opened his mouth to reveal a row of white baby teeth and gave a squeaky growl. His little paws trembled and he looked very weak and frightened.

"Stand back, please!" Mr. Pinch announced as the visitors pushed forward to get a better look. "Make way for the vet."

Zoe's mom knelt down slowly next to the cub. "There, there, little one. I'm not going to hurt you," she soothed as she examined the lion's eyes, ears, teeth, tummy, and paws. The cub shrank away, snarling as fiercely as he could. Zoe's mom looked up. "You found him just in time, Uncle Horace. It looks like he hasn't eaten in weeks."

Zoe and Meep shared a worried look. The cub seemed confused and very scared. He kept turning his head from side to side, as if he was looking for someone in the crowd. Zoe desperately wanted to explain that everyone at the Rescue Zoo was really kind and wanted to help him. But she couldn't talk to him in front of the crowd—she had to keep the animals' secret.

Zoe felt a gentle tug on her hair and realized it was Kiki trying to get her attention.

Great-Uncle Horace was standing next to her. Leaning closer, he whispered, "My dear, this little chap needs help. Will you promise to look after him for me?"

Zoe stared at her great-uncle and then nodded. "I promise. I'll try my very best to help the cub."